The Snow Queen

Written by Abie Longstaff
Illustrated by Michael Foreman

Kay and Gerda spent all their days side by side. But one day, some bad snow fell on Kay.

The wicked Snow Queen had put a spell on the snow.

The bad snow made Kay feel frosty
and mean.

"I don't want to play with you!"
Kay said to Gerda.

Kay was rude to Gerda and made her feel sad.

"I wish Kay was not so cross," she wept.

That night, the Snow Queen came for Kay. She took him away on her sled!

Gerda was at her window. She saw them go.

"No!" said Gerda. "I must save him!"

Gerda went into the dark woods, but soon she was lost. Flakes of snow hid the sled tracks. A creepy sound gave her a fright.

Up sprang a robber girl!

"Give me your bag!" she shouted.

Gerda burst into tears. She told the girl all about Kay.

The robber girl felt sad for Gerda.
"Follow me," she said. She led Gerda
to the Snow Queen's home.

8

Gerda did not want to go in by herself,
but she had to save Kay.

The moon was high in the sky. It lit
the way.

Gerda found Kay in a frosty room and wept with joy.

Her tears made the bad snow in Kay melt. He got hot again. The good Kay was back!

They began to run, but the Snow
Queen came after them with a scream.

"Stop!"

She went to grab Kay.

But he was too hot for the Snow Queen's hand! The heat burnt her and she had to let him go.

Gerda and Kay ran all the way home.

After that, Kay and Gerda spent all their days side by side again.

And the Snow Queen never ever came back.

A map

Ideas for reading

Written by Clare Dowdall, PhD
Lecturer and Primary Literacy Consultant

Learning objectives: *(reading objectives correspond with Blue band; all other objectives correspond with White band)* recognise and use alternative ways of pronouncing graphemes; read more challenging texts which can be decoded using their acquired phonic knowledge and skills, along with automatic recognition of high frequency words; explore how particular words are used; engage with books through exploring and enacting interpretations

Curriculum links: Science, Citizenship

Focus phonemes: ow, igh, ur

Fast words: one, some, their

Resources: pencils, paper, whiteboard

Word count: 292

Getting started

- Ask children if they have heard of "The Snow Queen" as a character or a story. Ask for ideas about what a snow queen might be like, and collect phrases and words on the whiteboard to describe her, e.g. icy, frosty, mean to people, beautiful.

- Look at the front cover. Read the title together and remind children of the *ow* phoneme. Ask children to suggest other words that contain this phoneme, e.g. show, blow. Focus on the image of the Snow Queen and discuss what her character might be like.

- Turn to the blurb and read the text. Identify Kay and Gerda in the illustration. Discuss why and where the Snow Queen might have taken Kay.

Reading and responding

- Ask children to read pp2–3 aloud as a group. Discuss what has happened so far in the story. Check that children understand that the Snow Queen has stopped Kay and Gerda being friends and playing together.

- Model reading the text aloud with expression. Remind children to reread sentences if they have to pause to sound out new words, and model doing this.